MEL BAY'S

GETTING TO.........

SLIDE GUITAR

by STEVE DAWSON

MEL BAY ®

1 2 3 4 5 6 7 8 9 0

Visit us on the Web at www.melbay.com — E-mail us at email@melbay.com

INTRODUCTION

Greetings! This book is meant to be a crash course in playing slide guitar in a blues context. It can be pretty easy to pick up the basics of playing slide, especially in an open tuning, and this book is designed to help you from the early stages through some fairly advanced techniques that will help you along as far as you wish to take it.

I wanted to write a book to teach the concepts of slide guitar that I've learned and developed from listening to and watching others play, as well as performing and writing my own material for quite a few years. Rather than transcribe solos and pieces by the great slide players, I wanted to look at the concepts involved - to teach you to play slide in a way that allows you to develop your own sound, or to be able to recognize styles and learn songs on your own. There are lots of great books filled with transcriptions of the classics, and while I borrow bits and pieces from lots of players for the exercises in this book, no one piece will be exactly like any old recordings.

I also wanted this book to teach you some basics of music theory that I'll be explaining in a slide-guitar context, but that you can take away with you and apply to any instrument.

Early on in writing this book, I decided to focus on open-G tuning. This is because I wanted to really dig into the techniques of playing slide guitar, without filling your head with too much information on tunings as well - there's enough information on other tunings to fill a few more volumes. The whole book is in open-G tuning, except for the final chapter, in which we'll look at some other tunings and their basics.

I also decided that I would base this whole book around simple blues applications. I play slide in settings from blues and bluegrass to jazz, country and Hawaiian music, and I write lots of material on slide guitar as well. How-

ever, my experience is that most people wanting to learn slide are doing so because of hearing the great blues players. Again, there are books to be written on working slide into different styles, but there just isn't room here. If you're

Photo by Mark Mushett

feeling adventurous, you can take the information from this book and apply it to whatever style of music that you like.

This book is written with the assumption that the reader has a grasp of the basic blues format and the chords involved. It would also be a good idea to be able to comprehend basic rhythmic notation, in order to interpret the exercises properly. Other than that, slide beginners can jump right in.

- Steve Dawson -

-Photos by Alice Dawson-

Visit www.blackhenmusic.com
for more info on Steve and his various recording/touring projects.

TABLE OF CONTENTS

STANDARD NOTATION

All examples in this book are written in standard notation and tablature. Because of the tuning used in this book, reading standard notation will be very difficult. It is included for ease of rhythmic clarity as well as a way to see which notes are being played, for the reader's interest.

ONE BAR IS DIVIDED INTO FOUR BEATS (IN 4/4 TIME):

ONE WHOLE NOTE EQUALS FOUR BEATS:

ONE HALF NOTE EQUALS TWO BEATS:

ONE QUARTER NOTE EQUALS ONE BEAT:

ONE EIGHTH NOTE EQUALS HALF OF ONE BEAT:

ONE SIXTEENTH NOTE EQUALS ONE QUARTER OF ONE BEAT:

Each of the previous examples have equivalent rests:

ONE WHOLE NOTE REST EQUALS FOUR BEATS:

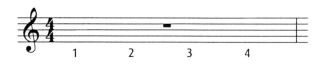

ONE HALF NOTE REST EQUALS TWO BEATS:

ONE QUARTER NOTE REST EQUALS ONE BEAT:

ONE EIGHTH NOTE REST EQUALS HALF OF ONE BEAT:

ONE SIXTEENTH NOTE REST EQUALS ONE QUARTER OF ONE BEAT:

TRIPLETS

THREE QUARTER NOTE TRIPLETS FIT EQUALLY INTO TWO BEATS:

THREE EIGHTH NOTE TRIPLETS FIT EQUALLY INTO ONE BEAT:

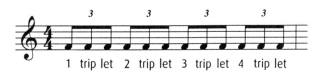

TABLATURE

In tablature, each horizontal line represents a guitar string. The top line is the 1st string (high string) and the bottom line is the 6th string (low string). The number on the line is the number of the fret to be played. Tablature will not provide any rhythmic information - look at the standard notation for rhythmic information.

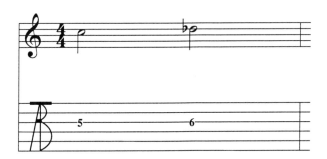

FINGERINGS

There will be very little fingering information in this book. For the left-hand, either you will be using the slide, or very basic left-hand fingerings that will not require specific notation. Chapter 4 deals with a specific right-hand technique and in some of the exercises, right-hand fingerings will be specified by **t** for the thumb, **i** for the index finger, **m** for the middle finger, and **a** for the ring finger.

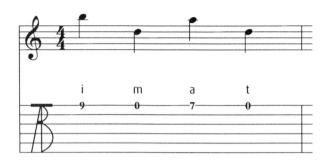

In the case of two notes being played together, if there is a down-stemmed note, it is played with the right-hand thumb, and up-stems are played with right-hand fingers.

ARTICULATION

There are a number of specific slide and non-slide articulations used in this book.

An **H** indicates a hammer-on. This would only happen between an open string and a slide note. The open string is played, and then the slide hits the string without the right-hand picking again. A **P** indicates a pull-off. In this case, you would play a slide note, and pull the slide off letting the open string ring.

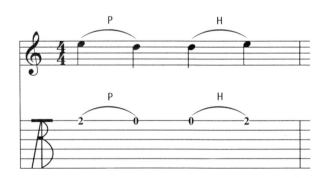

A tied note is simply a note that is held in value over a barline, or through the middle of a bar. Since there is no new pitch, or slide activity, the tablature will not indicate any changes.

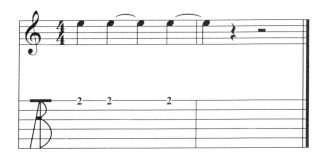

When there is a tied note and the pitch changes, there will be an **S** over the tie to indicate the slide. Slide to the second note without picking again, but let each note ring out for its full value.

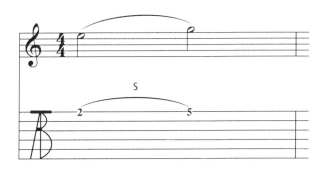

Every fretted note will automatically be played with the slide. An upward arrow indicates that you would slide from a lower fret (usually one or two frets, but it's not important to be from any specific note) into the indicated fret. A down slide indicates that you would play the note for almost it's full value before letting the slide descend by a fret or two.

A downward slide into a note (less common) indicates that you would slide into the designated fret from a fret or two above the note.

The left-hand fingers are used only when there is an **NS** (no slide) written above the tablature. The fingers continue until the dotted line ends.

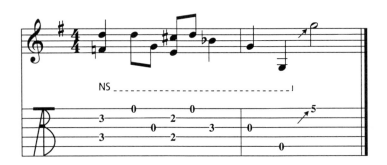

CHORD SYMBOLS

Chord symbols are included over the full-length pieces. Most of the chords are very simple and will be explained in Chapter 1. When there are other specific chords to be played, chord diagrams will be supplied.

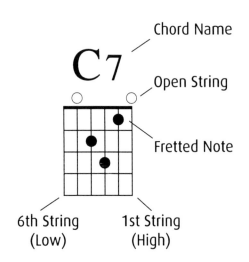

CHAPTER 1: OPEN-G TUNING

I'm choosing to spend the largest amount of time in this book focussed on open-G tuning, both because of its similarities to standard guitar tuning (three of the strings stay the same from standard tuning), and because of its sonic characteristics - the growling lower strings, the easy access to very low notes and octaves, and the ease in which you can switch between playing both in a major tonality, or with a darker minor sound - these are all advantages when it comes to playing blues. There are a few ways to tune your guitar to an open-G chord, but for this book you'll be lowering three of the strings to different pitches.

TO GET TO OPEN-G TUNING FROM STANDARD TUNING

Remember that in this book, the 1st string refers to the **high** string; the 6th string is the **low** string!

USING A TUNER:

1) Tune the 1st string (the high one) down from E to D
2) Tune the 5th string down from A to G
3) Tune the 6th string down from E to D

Track #1

Your overall tuning will now be (from Low to High): **D G D G B D**

USING YOUR EAR AND/OR ADJACENT STRINGS AS REFERENCE:

(You should be able to identify the sound of an octave, and be able to play a (*)12th fret harmonic in order to be able to do this - check photo below for help with this if you need it.)

1) Play the 4th (D) string, let it ring, and then play the 1st string along with it. Tune the 1st string down until it lands an octave above the open 4th string (it will go down one whole-step from standard tuning). You can check it by playing the 3rd fret, 2nd string against the open 1st string - they should be the same, **or** play the 12th fret harmonic on the 4th string (see photo below) and make sure it sounds the same as the open 1st string.

(*) To get a harmonic at the 12th fret, touch, but don't press the string directly above the 12th fret, pick quite hard with your right hand, close to the bridge, and as soon as the string is ringing, take your left finger off. Refer to the photo above.

9

2) Play the 3rd (G) string, let it ring, and then play the 5th string along with it. Tune the 5th string down until it lands an octave below the open 3rd string. You can check it by playing the (*)12th fret harmonic on the 5th string against the open 3rd string - they should be the same.

3) Play the 4th string again, let it ring, and then play the 6th string along with it. Tune the 6th string down until it lands an octave below the open 4th string. You can check it by playing the 12th fret harmonic on the 6th string against the open 4th string - they should be the same.

Your overall tuning will now be (from low to high): **D G D G B D**

Strum all six strings together - you should have a zesty G major chord begging to be slid upon!

CHORD SHAPES

Here are some chord shapes for a few standard open position chords (played with fingers). Notice the similarities between these chords and the same chords as you would play them in standard tuning: the middle three strings are the same. Try and get the hang of playing these chords. Some of them aren't full six-string chords anymore, like they were in standard tuning (the A7, for example). Try to avoid strumming any strings that have an **X**.

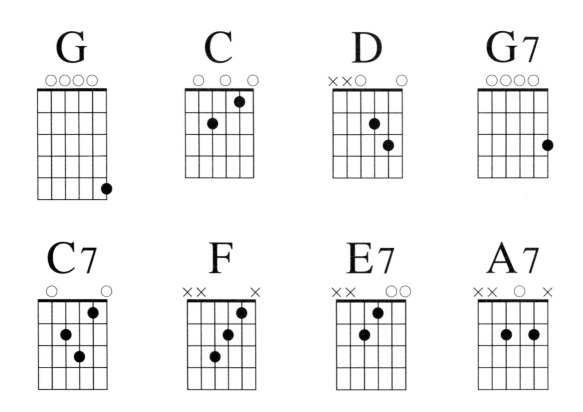

(*) See photo previous page.

CHAPTER 2: BASIC SLIDE SETUP AND TECHNIQUE

In this chapter we'll look at the most basic left and right-hand techniques that you need to know to be able to play slide. However, before we get into that, there are a number of considerations for the tools you'll use - your guitar and your slide.

GUITAR SETUP

Ideally, you'll have one guitar devoted to slide - setting up a guitar exclusively for slide playing is something to consider for a number of reasons. First of all, a well-setup slide guitar will be difficult to play regular guitar on. Another reason is that almost any old guitar can make a great slide guitar - common problems that cheap old guitars have (bad action, intonation, worn-out frets) are not going to cause as much of a problem when playing slide. A good slide setup will have slightly higher action than a normal guitar, heavier strings (on acoustics I'd recommend at least a .14 gauge for the 1st string, down to a .56 or heavier on the 6th string. On electrics you could even go heavier), and a flatter radius than on a normal guitar also helps (this means that the strings are in a straighter and flatter line against the fretboard, as opposed to curving along with the neck). There are plenty of old used guitars lying around stores for around $150 that might be perfect - there's no need to spend a huge bundle of cash in getting a good sounding slide guitar. Some of the old acoustic brands worth checking around used shops for include Kay, Stella, and Harmony. Kay, Harmony and Silvertone also made some funky electric guitars that are perfect for slide. Of course, you can also still find good deals on higher end guitars, and resonator instruments, but a Rolls Royce of guitars is not required for playing slide.

THE SLIDE

There are many kinds of slides available on the market. They come in all sizes and are generally made from metal, glass, or porcelain. The kind of slide you buy really depends on comfort and the kind of tone you prefer. I like the sound of glass for bottleneck style playing. I find that metal is a bit too brittle, but then again there are a lot of slide players who use metal slides whose sound I like, so it just depends on what feels right. I suggest trying different kinds and seeing what you prefer. I would recommend something with some weight to it - there are glass slides that are so thin and light you can barely feel them. To develop good tone and vibrato you need to have a slide that you can really feel on your finger and that has some substantial mass.

BASIC SLIDE TECHNIQUE - RIGHT HAND

I strongly recommend playing fingerstyle when you start playing slide. The right hand can get quite involved, and to be a good slide player, you'll need to be playing and muting strings with more than just a flatpick. Some players successfully incorporate a combination of flatpick and fingers, but just by holding a pick between your thumb and index finger, you're eliminating the use of one digit. If you're just beginning, try starting out with fingerstyle. As far as fingerstyle goes, you can play with bare fingers, a thumbpick, or thumb and fingerpicks – this is also a personal choice that is best to experiment with to find what's the most comfortable for you. I use a plastic thumbpick and sometimes three metal fingerpicks (with holes in the fingertips to feel the strings through) – because the acoustic guitar is a relatively quiet instrument, fingerpicks allow you to get some more volume out of your guitar. If you're playing a resonator guitar, using fingerpicks is the best way to get the most response out of your instrument. Electric players might find that bare fingers work better, as volume isn't an issue.

LEFT HAND

I recommend putting the slide on your pinky. This leaves you with three other fingers to fret chords, play notes without the slide and to mute the strings behind the slide. You'll notice in the above photo that my index finger points off into outer space – this is just a strange habit of mine that has no effect on the tone or any muting.

BASIC SLIDE TECHNIQUES

The first step is to get comfortable using the slide – try playing these chords by laying the slide flat across all six strings and just strum the full chord with your right hand, or pick several notes with any right hand fingers as you pass through these positions.

2-A – THE BASIC SLIDE CHORDS:

Slide at the 3rd fret = B♭

Slide at the 5th fret = C

Slide at the 7th fret = D

Slide at the 10th fret = F

Slide at the 12th fret = G

Here is a checklist of basic left-hand techniques:

1) **Keep your left hand relaxed** – You want to make sure that you're not pressing the slide down too much as you play, or you'll get lots of nasty fret noise. The slide should touch the strings, but there's not much pressure needed to get a good sound.

2) **Land directly on top of the fret** - In normal guitar playing, you're always shooting to have your left-hand fingers land close behind, but not on, the fret you're playing. With slide, it's a little different. When you slide over the strings, the frets become nothing more than reference points – the slide essentially becomes a moveable fret. So, always aim to land directly on top of the fret indicated by the music.

3) **Keep the slide directly perpendicular to the neck** - If it is not in a straight line, you will be out of tune when you are playing more than one string at a time.

4) **Your thumb should act as an anchor** - When you get to the fret that you're shooting for, your left-hand thumb should stay firmly against the neck, and the arch into your index finger should not make contact. This will help with your intonation and later, your vibrato.

Refer to these photographs and keep sliding between all of these chords. Try sliding into the chord from one fret lower, then two frets, and then three frets. Playing slide is very subjective, because when you slide into a note, you can start from very close to the target note, or way down the neck – let your impeccable taste decide...

Once you're comfortable playing these full chords, you should start to play some single notes and try to develop some vibrato. Notes on the 1st string are the easiest to play, because you can angle the slide away from the neck after it makes contact with the 1st string. This allows you to play one note without interference from other strings (see photo below).

Try this next exercise, which is just a series of slides into the same note.

2-B – 1ST STRING SLIDES:

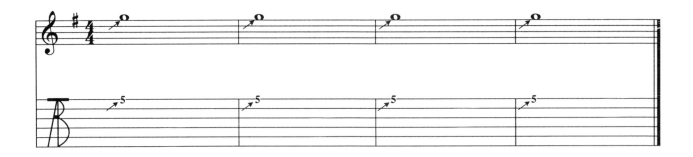

At first, play the 5th fret with your finger to get the pitch of the note firmly in your head. Then when you use the slide to get to the note, you'll have a reference point of where you want to end up. It's like target practice – it will take a while to train your hand to get to the note and slam on the brakes before you end up too sharp.

This next exercise is written exactly the same as **2-B**, but this time, try sliding into the notes from various frets below. Listen to the audio example for a few variations. The note you slide from will never be specified – this is up to you to play by what feels right...

2-C – MORE 1ST STRING SLIDES:

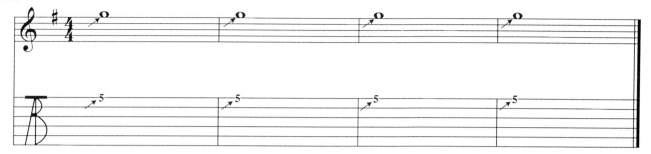

Now try the exact same thing, but slide into the note from above.

2-D – SLIDING FROM ABOVE:

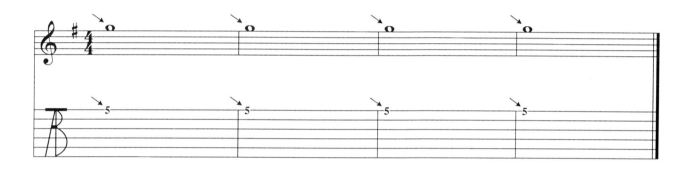

VIBRATO

Vibrato is another important element of slide playing that takes a lot of time to develop. To start adding vibrato to a note, use your left-hand thumb as an anchor on the back of the neck. Keep your wrist relaxed and shake your left hand gently, not letting the slide lift off the string. This is where a heavier weight slide can really help – it will provide some momentum to keep a long, consistent vibrato going. I left the vibrato out of the music altogether – it's something that you can use as a flavour. It doesn't always have to be there, and it can be done so many ways, that once you get used to doing it, you can add it in anytime and in any way you choose.

Once again, we'll use the same example, but this time experiment with different styles of vibrato. This is a very simple exercise, but you should spend some time listening to this audio example and trying to perfect a smooth vibrato.

2-E – FUN WITH VIBRATO:

Now, try some vibrato after sliding into the note from above...

2-F – VIBRATO AFTER SLIDING FROM ABOVE:

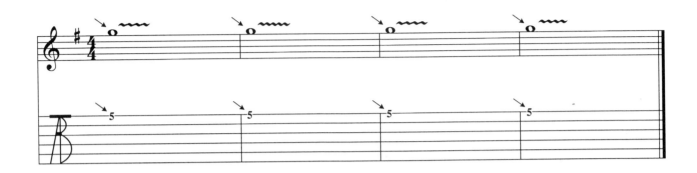

Now we'll try sliding into a few different notes on the 1st string. Keep your slide angled away from the strings after it makes contact with the 1st, just to avoid excess string noise. Again, play this with your left-hand fingers first, in order to memorize the sound, and then play it with the slide, focusing on **intonation** (playing notes properly in tune) and vibrato.

Track #4

2-G – COMBINING SLIDE NOTES WITH OPEN STRINGS:

Spend some time with these basics, and keep checking yourself to make sure you've got the techniques down before moving on to the next chapters.

CHAPTER 3 – INTRODUCING AND BUILDING ON THE BLUES PROGRESSION

(ALSO INTRODUCING SOME BASIC THEORY THAT EVERYONE SHOULD KNOW)

The blues progression has countless variations, feels, rhythms and tempos. However, we're going to break it down to its simplest form in this chapter and look at how it relates to open-G tuning. Most of what you learn in this chapter will be using your left-hand fingers as opposed to the slide. You'll learn the basics of this tuning, how to make the necessary chords, and start to be able to navigate the fretboard successfully.

CHORDS

The most basic form of blues usually consists of three chords (in some cases, such as the music of Robert Pete Williams, Blind Willie Johnson, John Lee Hooker and others, there might only be one chord). These three chords are usually referred to as the **I**, **IV** and **V** chords. This numeric system of naming chords makes transposing a song into a different key quite easy. Here's how it works:

The major scale consists of 7 notes. For most of this book, we're in the key of G, so let's look at the notes of the G major scale: **G A B C D E F♯**

If we assign a number to each degree of the scale, the result is:

G = **I**
A = **II**
B = **III**
C = **IV**
D = **V**
E = **VI**
F♯ = **VII**

So in the key of G, a progression containing the **I**, **IV**, and **V** chords would contain the chords G, C and D.

One more example – the key of C:

C = **I**
D = **II**
E = **III**
F = **IV**
G = **V**
A = **VI**
B = **VII**

So in the key of C, the **I**, **IV**, **V** progression would contain the chords C, F, and G

At this stage, there are two types of chords you should know how to play – the major chord, and the 7th chord. The **major chord** is a three-note chord (a triad), but on the guitar, it's quite normal to play one or more of those three notes more than once, because you have six strings at your disposal. For example, if you play all six strings of the open-G tuned guitar, you're actually only playing three different notes (two G's, three D's and a B). The **7th chord** adds one more note onto the triad to make a four-note chord. You'll see these chords written as G7, C7, D7, etc. The note that you're adding is the **flat 7** of the key and has a very bluesy quality to it. You'll be seeing lots of 7th chords in this book.

Here are the basic forms of the major chords in open G, played with 1st, 2nd and 3rd fingers (no slide).

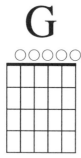 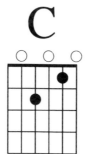 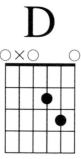

And a couple of variations:

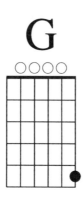 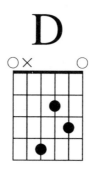

And now the 7th chords:

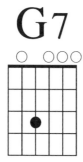 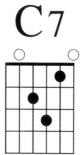 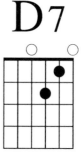

A simple layout for a 12-bar blues progression, with the chords from the key of G plugged into it, is:

3-A – Strumming Chords Through a Blues Progression:

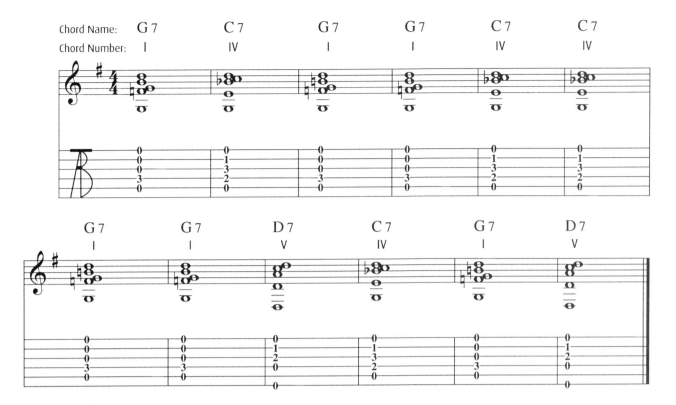

With the slide, you can also find the major chords for the **I** chord at the 12th fret, the **IV** chord at the 5th fret, and the **V** chord at the 7th fret.

Using the progression from exercise **3-A**, we'll go through the example using the slide to play these same chords, strumming or picking any group of notes on beat 1 of each bar.

3-A2 – Strumming or Picking the Slide Chords From **3-A** (Audio-Only Exercise)
Track #5

Swing vs. Straight Rhythm

The two most common types of rhythms you'll encounter are swing and straight rhythms. They look the same on paper, but they're played with a different feel. Straight rhythm gives equal value to two 8th notes in a beat, as in this example:

3-B – Straight Rhythm:
Track #6

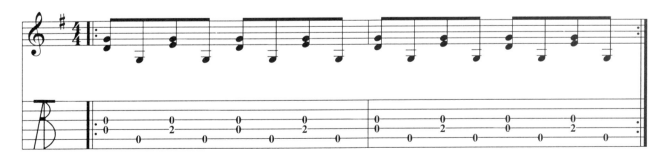

Swing rhythm shifts the feel, so that the first 8th note is longer, and the second shorter – the two together equal the same total amount of time as the two straight 8th notes, but with a different feel.

3-C – SWING RHYTHM:

Track #7

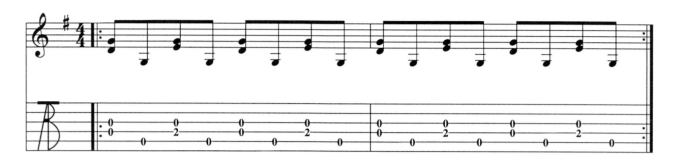

Throughout this book, some examples will use swing rhythm and some will use straight. You can practice them either way, but when you listen to the audio to go along with each exercise, try and distinguish between the two types.

Now we'll apply some basic rhythm patterns to these chords and throw them into the same progression (you'll notice that this progression has a swing feel to it). In this next example, I've come up with a basic one-bar pattern for each chord, with slight variations at the tail end of each one. By using the basic 12-bar progression that we've already established, I've pasted together an entire rhythm pattern to cover the whole progression. Since there are only three chords, there are really only three different rhythm patterns to learn – one for the **I** chord, one for the **IV** chord, and one for the **V** chord. This entire example is played without the slide – first of all let's break this down into three different one-bar patterns (one for each different chord). To learn these patterns, take some time to get the fingering right slowly, and then **loop** the pattern (repeat it over and over) until you feel comfortable playing it.

3-D – PATTERN FOR THE G7 OR I CHORD:

Track #8

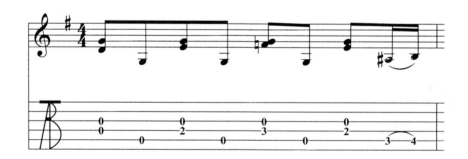

3-E – PATTERN FOR THE C7 OR IV CHORD (THIS PATTERN LEADS STRAIGHT BACK INTO 3-D):

Track #9

20

3-F – Pattern for the D7 or V Chord (This Pattern Leads Straight Back Into 3-E):

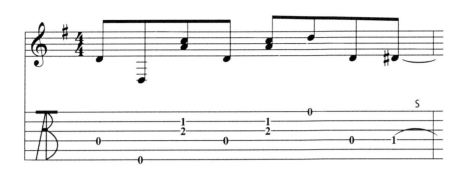

Now we'll just take those examples, and with a few slight variations, just cut and paste them into a standard 12-bar progression (remember that this is all done without the slide)...

3-G – 12-Bar Blues Using Repeated Rhythm Patterns (No Slide):

21

Another common element of the blues is the **turnaround**. This is usually a two-bar pattern that takes up the last bars of the progression. In the example we're using, it would replace the **I** and **V** chords in bars 11 and 12. Here are three turnarounds to try (again, all without the slide). Don't let these examples intimidate you – they may look daunting at first, but just go to the audio example and learn how they should sound. Then, start to play them slowly.

3-H – TURNAROUND #1:
Track #12

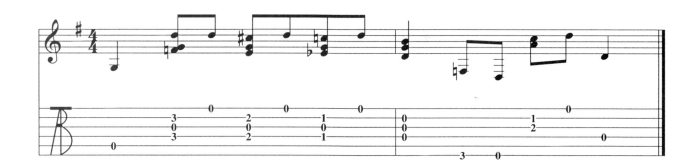

3-I – TURNAROUND #2:
Track #13

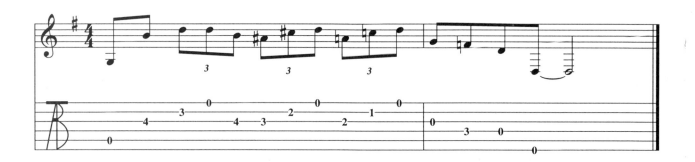

3-J – TURNAROUND #3:
Track #14

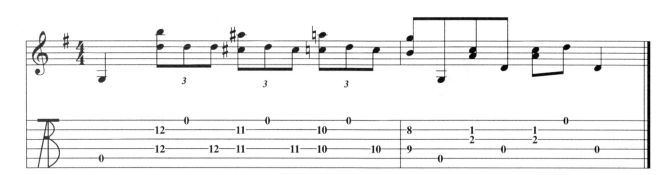

After you have these down, go back to Exercise **3-G** and replace the last two bars with these, one at a time.

Variations on a Theme

The progression we've been working on is by no means the only blues form you'll encounter. Hopefully, by memorizing the various chords, positions, numbers and rhythms, you'll be able to apply them to many different forms. You'll find that most people in a jamming or rehearsing situation will use the number system to outline the songs' chord changes. Here are a couple of progressions that you should try to play. Start by cutting and pasting exercises **3-D**, **3-E** and **3-F** into these progressions. On the audio CD, I'll play through each progression using the chords from this chapter, and then I'll improvise over top of the progression so you can get a feel for how these sound. On these simple charts, each chord numeral represents one bar of music.

 **3-K** – Variation on a 12-Bar Blues:
Track #15

I	IV	I	I	IV	IV	I	I	V	V	I	I

 **3-L** – Standard 8-bar blues:
Track #16

I	V	IV	IV	I	V	I	I

CHAPTER 4 – LEFT AND RIGHT-HAND MUTING TECHNIQUES

While you might want to sometimes use a loose, open sound, muting with both the left and right hand is integral to getting a precise, clean slide tone. It involves blocking strings that are not being played, but that the slide is passing over.

LEFT HAND

The left hand can effectively dampen strings by placing the fingers behind the slide flat against the strings. This can provide support, and help with intonation as well, but its main purpose is to get rid of unwanted harmonics that come through behind the slide as it touches the strings. From now on, remind yourself to keep your first three left-hand fingers (assuming your slide is on your pinky) straight and flat against the strings as you slide. You don't need to apply much pressure, just make contact with the strings.

RIGHT HAND

The right hand is much more involved and the rest of the chapter will be devoted to developing this technique.

This technique is based on using the thumb and first three fingers as a moveable unit (this certainly isn't the only way to do it, but it seems to work!).

POSITION 1

To start, we'll go to the top two strings. In this exercise, the notes alternate from the 2nd to 1st string. Use your right-hand thumb for the 2nd string, and index finger for the 1st. As you play the 2nd string with your thumb, touch the 1st string with your index finger. Then, as you strike the 1st string, bring your thumb back down to rest on the 2nd string at the same time. The result will be two distinct notes that do not overlap.

We'll call this **right-hand position 1**.

4-A – POSITION 1:
Track #17

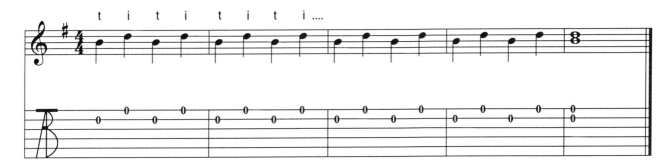

Try not to cut off the note early – let each note ring right up until you play the next one. Now we'll incorporate the slide. Instead of covering all six strings, move the slide off the neck until it only touches the top two or three strings (see photo).

This will eliminate the need for muting more than one string at a time. In the next exercise, use the exact right-hand fingering from exercise **4-A**, up until the last note, at which time you'll play both strings together (still with thumb and index).

4-B – POSITION 1 WITH SLIDE:
Track #18

POSITION 2

Next, we'll move down to the 2nd and 3rd strings. Since the slide will now be moving across the top three strings, but you don't want to hear the 1st string, you'll need to mute the 1st string with your right-hand middle finger. Also, you'll notice that the notes aren't all in the same fret from bar to bar as in exercise 4-B. In the tiny gap between playing one string and muting the next, move the slide to the next note. You should try to do this so that you can't hear the slide to the next note.

 4-C – POSITION 2:
Track #19

 4-D – MORE POSITION 2:
Track #20

Now we'll use the thumb and two fingers to play the top three strings. In this example, let the first two notes of each bar ring out together, then as you play the 3rd string with the thumb, dampen the top two strings – index finger on the 2nd string, middle finger on the 1st string. On the last note, slide to the 5th fret of the 1st string, but angle the slide away from the strings after it makes contact with the 1st. This will allow you to hear both the slide note and the open 3rd string together.

26

4-E – POSITION 2, USING THUMB AND TWO FINGERS:

Track #21

POSITION 3

In this exercise, we'll move between the 3rd and 4th strings. Use your thumb for the 4th string, index for 3rd, while keeping your middle finger on the 2nd string and ring finger on the 1st. The slide should just be far enough across the strings to cover the first four.

4-F – RIGHT-HAND POSITION 3:

Track #22

Position 4

Use the same idea as positions 1, 2 and 3, but move your right hand down to the 5th, 4th, and 3rd strings.

4-G – Right-Hand Position 4:
Track #23

Position 5

Once again – the same concept, with the right hand moving down to the 6th, 5th and 4th strings.

4-H – RIGHT-HAND POSITION 5:

Now that you've got the idea of how it feels to have your fingers moving in this group (thumb, index, middle each assigned to an adjacent string), we'll look at a more musical example of how this would be used. We'll start in position one, and move through various positions, until we end up on position five (with your thumb on the 6th string, index on 5th, middle on 4th, etc.). Watch the position markings below the music for the timing of the right-hand position changes, and pay attention to the right-hand fingerings above the tablature. This is a lot of information, but once you get it, you'll start to be able to mute strings without thinking about any of this...

4-I – RIGHT HAND MOVING THROUGH ALL 5 MUTING POSITIONS:

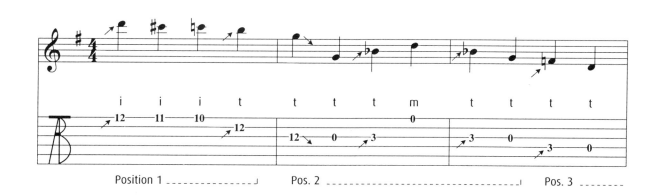

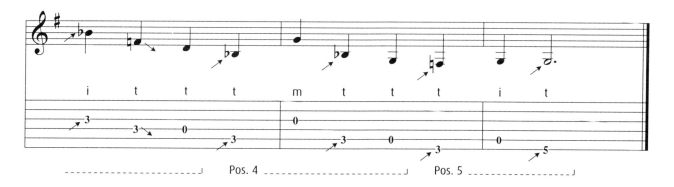

Now we'll look at muting in the context of a blues progression – keep in mind that the notes here are fairly simple – it's the right-hand muting you want to concentrate on! If you can get the hang of playing a piece like this, you'll find that your hand will be accustomed to the shape and you'll be able to apply this technique to the rest of the chapters.

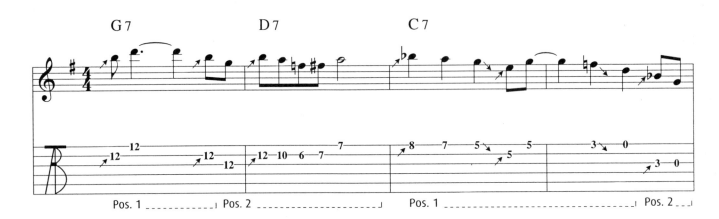

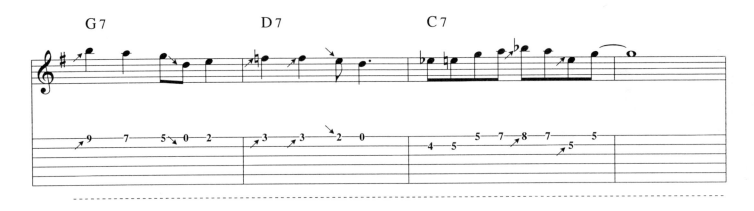

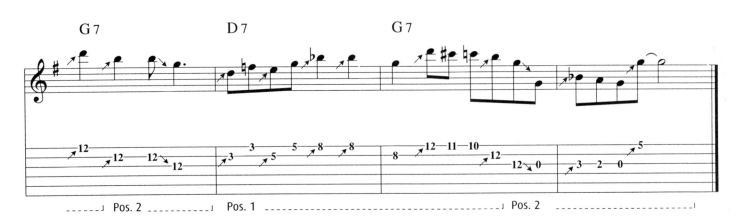

Here's another example of muting, this time I haven't specified the fingerings – try to work it out for yourself, using the right-hand positions from this chapter.

4-K

Track #27

Master these exercises so that your right hand automatically starts to make these moves. Soon you'll be muting up a storm...

CHAPTER 5 – PLAYING IN THE KEY OF G

Since this book focuses on open-G tuning, we'll spend a good deal of time now looking at the key of G. In this key, you have the advantage of being able to use all of the open strings. This is comparable to a blues guitarist playing in the key of E on a standard tuned guitar – while a lot of what you play can be transferred to other keys, there are a great deal of extra licks and techniques at your disposal. In this chapter we'll look at the basics of approaching a blues progression in the key of G, utilizing the open strings, and the main positions for the chords involved. Later on, we'll also look at a G minor blues progression.

In Chapter 6, we'll look at some more complex scales that can be used, but for this chapter, we'll learn some basic shapes and patterns that work in the key of G.

Here's a simple shape to learn that works well in the key of G.

5-A – BASIC G SHAPE:
Track #28

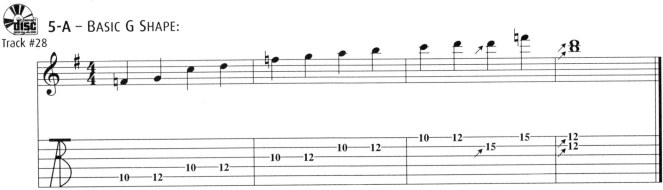

You'll notice that this is based around the 12th fret. The 12th fret on the guitar is where you reach the octave, so since the open strings are a G chord, the 12th fret is a G chord as well.

The notes from the 10th and 15th frets come from various forms of the blues scale and can be used for effective slide licks. Here are a few to try.

5-B - BASIC G LICKS BASED AROUND 12TH FRET POSITION:
Track #29

5-C – BASIC G LICKS CONT.:
Track #30

32

5-D – BASIC G LICKS CONT.:

As for the open position of G, learn this pattern.

5-E – BASIC G SHAPE, OPEN POSITION:

At the end of that pattern, you end up at the 5th fret, 1st string. Make sure that your slide is angled so that it only touches the 1st string. If you are covering more strings, you will make it sound like you're playing a C chord (the chord that the slide makes when covering the 5th fret), and since this exercise is meant for a G chord, you'll want to make sure that doesn't happen.

Once you feel comfortable with these licks, try making some up of your own, and improvising using these shapes. **5-B** – **5-D** all ended on the 3rd string, 12th fret – the root note. This is a very safe place to end up, but also try ending on different notes at the 12th fret – they'll all work!

This same position and the previous set of licks can also be transferred directly to the other chords. By moving to the 5th fret, you'll be at the **IV** chord, and by moving to the 7th fret, you'll be at the **V** chord (if you have any confusion about what these chords and numerals mean, refer back to Chapter 3).

5-F - EX. 5-A TRANSPOSED TO THE IV CHORD (C):

5-G - Ex. 5-A TRANSPOSED TO THE **V** Chord (D):

As we looked at in chapter 3, the basic blues progression consists of 12 bars. Here is a possible layout for the chords (each numeral represents one bar of music).

I	I	I	I	IV	IV	I	I	V	IV	I	I

The first way that we'll approach this is to come up with a two-bar lick for the G chord, and a two-bar lick for the C chord.

5-H - LICK FOR THE G, OR **I** CHORD:

5-I - LICK FOR THE C OR **IV** CHORD:

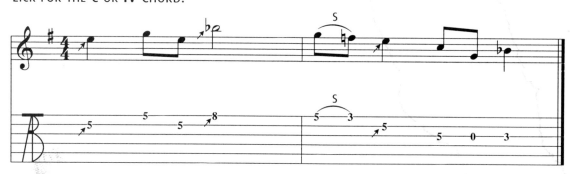

Using these licks, we'll be able to play through the first eight bars of the progression. Then we'll hit the **V** and **IV** chords that change after one bar, so here are some licks that will work for them.

5-J - LICK FOR ONE BAR OF THE **D** OR **V** CHORD:

5-K - LICK FOR THE ONE BAR OF THE C OR IV CHORD:

That leaves us with the two-bar turnaround, which we learned in Chapter 3. Refer back to **3-H**, **3-I** and **3-J** if you need to refresh your memory.

Now we'll put these all together over the blues progression. Notice that I've indicated which lick we are using over each bar.

 5-L – PIECING TOGETHER **5-H** THROUGH **5-K**:

Track #33

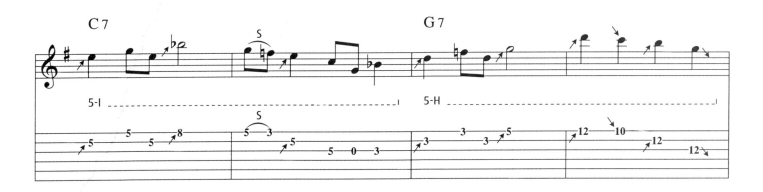

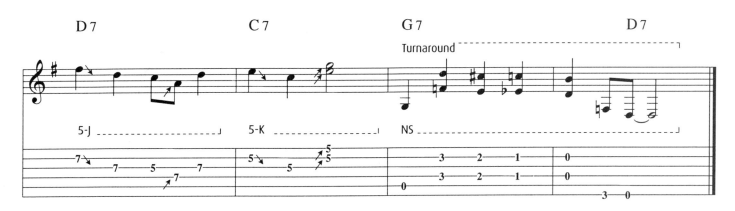

35

Now try this same concept with a slight variation to the progression; in the last four bars, we'll stay on the **V** chord (at the 7th fret) for two bars, and will resolve straight to the **I** chord turnaround, instead of going to the **IV** chord. This is one of countless variations on the blues progression.

It looks like this:

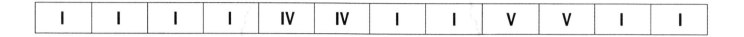

The licks in this exercise are different from the ones in **5-L**, but still based on the patterns we learned, and still just one simple idea transposed to all three chords.

 5-M – ANOTHER BLUES PROGRESSION USING REPEATED PHRASES:
Track #34

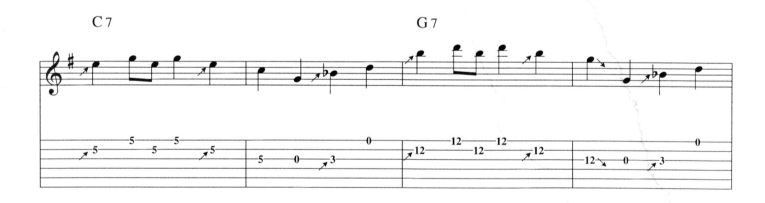

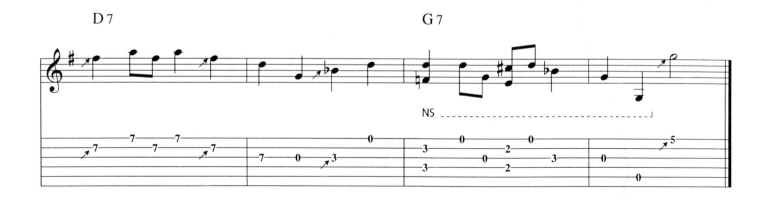

Playing in G Minor

Now we'll take a look at a minor-based blues progression. The chords are still the **I**, **IV**, and **V**, but in this example the **I** and **IV** chords will be minor.

5-N – Chords For Playing G-Minor Blues:

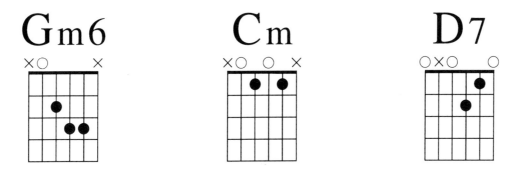

Take some time to learn the chords in this progression and play along with the recording (see audio exercise **5-R**) before you tackle the whole exercise.

The main difference between playing in a minor key and a major key is one particular note – the 3rd. When you play the open 2nd string in this tuning (B), you're playing the major 3rd, which defines the sound as major. If you are tuned like this and want to play in a minor key, you must avoid this note – menacing glances will be shot your way from fellow musicians at a rehearsal or jam session if you are playing the major 3rd over a minor chord, so for your personal safety, let's look at how to play out of the positions we've learned in this chapter, but altering that one pesky note so that it works in a minor context.

At the 12th fret position you will find the minor 3rd at the 11th fret, 2nd string.

5-O - G Minor 12th Fret Position:

Track #35

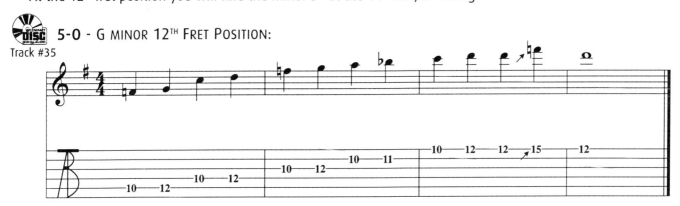

In the open position, you will find the minor 3rd at the 3rd fret, 3rd and 5th strings.

5-P - G Minor Open Position

Track #36

To play over a C minor chord, change the 5th fret, 2nd string to the 4th fret.

 5-Q - C MINOR POSITION FOR THE **IV** CHORD
Track #37

Since the **V** chord in this progression is major, we can keep the same positions from before (ex. **5-G**) for that chord.

Now let's apply these concepts to a minor progression.

 5-R – G-MINOR BLUES PROGRESSION:
Track #38

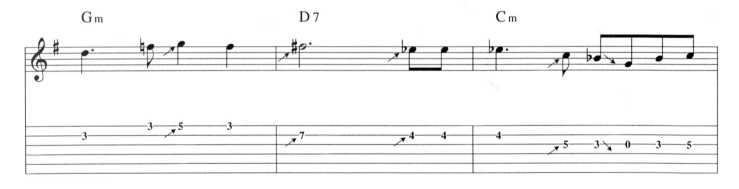

38

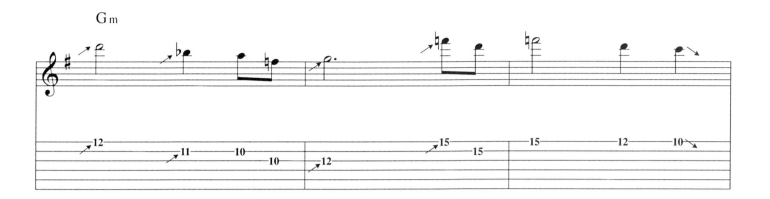

By now, you should have a grasp on how to find your way through a simple blues progression. Try to take some of these examples and expand on them, as well as using the audio examples to begin improvising using the tools you've learned.

CHAPTER 6 – GOING FURTHER INTO THE KEY OF G

So far, much of the playing we've done has been based out of simple positions that essentially shifted for each chord of the progression. In this chapter we'll get more in depth with some ways to approach playing blues with slide and look in-depth at two types of scales – the **minor blues scale**, and the **major blues scale** (also called the **Mixolydian mode**). This chapter will introduce you to these scales, and the rest of the book will continue to use them.

Before we start looking at the scales, let's get really familiar with the tuning and the fingerboard. Here are the notes that are available on the open strings:

       1st String = D (5th degree of G scale)

       2nd String = B (3rd degree of G scale)

       3rd String = G (1st degree of G scale)

       4th String = D (5th degree of G scale)

       5th String = G (1st degree of G scale)

       6th String = D (5th degree of G scale)

You can see that there are only three different notes between the six strings. This makes things easy for learning scales on individual strings. Since we only have three different notes between all the strings, there are only three different patterns to learn for playing a scale up and down individual strings.

It's also a good idea to be acquainted with your available root notes. A root note is the note of the key you are in – in this case, it's G. In this example, we'll locate the various G's around the neck up to the 12th fret.

6-A - LOCATION OF G NOTES BETWEEN OPEN STRINGS AND 12TH FRET:

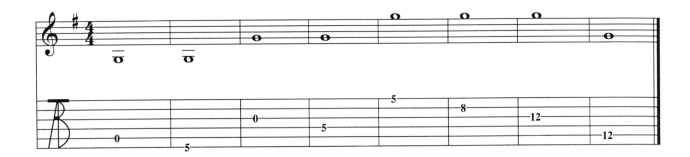

By keeping track of where you are in relation to these root notes, you can give yourself a grounding point, or somewhere to return to which will make the fretboard seem much less daunting.

Listen to the tonal differences of the same note played in different octaves and on different strings. For example, bars 5 and 8 are exactly the same note, but on the guitar they sound quite different.

G Scales

Now we'll learn the two scales that will be the focus for the rest of the book. The **minor-blues** scale is the minor-pentatonic scale (a common five-note scale) with the addition of one **blue note**, while the **Mixolydian** mode is almost identical to the major scale (a seven-note scale), except for the alteration of one note that gives the scale a bluesy quality. Between these two scales, you can cover most of the ground found in different styles of blues playing (as well as a lot of country, jazz, rock, etc.). Always refer back to this section if you find yourself confused about what the scales are or if you feel lost on the fretboard.

Minor Blues Scale

The minor blues scale is a six-note scale that contains these notes in the key of G:

G Bb C C# D F

First we'll look at the scale in the open position.

 6-B - G-MINOR BLUES SCALE IN OPEN POSITION:
Track #39

 6-C - G-MINOR BLUES SCALE AT THE 12TH FRET:
Track #40

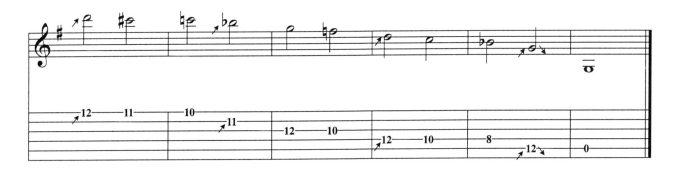

41

Now that you are familiar with the sound of the minor blues scale, we'll learn it going up each string from the open string to the 12th fret. Remember that even though we'll look at the scale on each string, there are only three different patterns to learn because there are only three different open string notes! The next three exercises will show you the blues scale going up the 6th, 4th and 1st strings, but because they're all D strings, it's really just the same pattern.

6-D - G-Minor Blues Scale on the 6th String:

6-E - G-Minor Blues Scale on the 4th String:

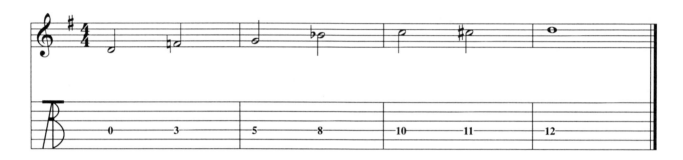

6-F - G-Minor Blues Scale on the 1st String:

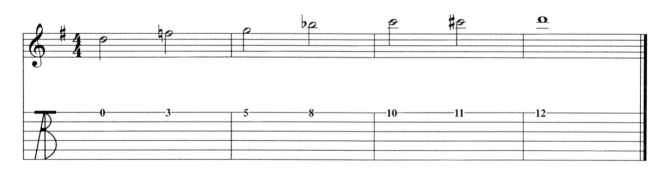

Now we'll check out the same thing on the 3rd and 5th strings.

6-G - G-Minor Blues Scale on the 5th String:

6-H - G-Minor Blues Scale on the 3rd String:

And finally, the lone 2nd string. This is the one string that we won't use the open string – in the key of G, this note is the major 3rd, and that note is not in this minor blues scale.

6-I - G-Minor Blues Scale on the 2nd String:

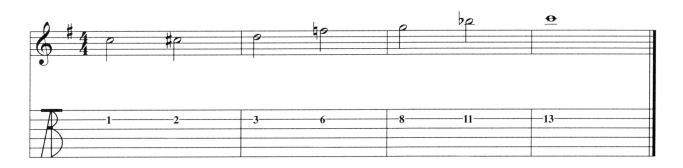

Now let's tie these all in and play a tune, using the G-minor blues scale in these positions.

6-J

Track #41

G 7

MAJOR-BLUES, OR MIXOLYDIAN MODE

Harmonically, a simple blues can get quite complex. Aside from the G-minor blues scale, there's also a major-based blues scale that's very useful. This is also known as the Mixolydian mode and is the ideal scale to use with 7th chords (the chords that appear all over these blues progressions we're dealing with). You'll notice that most of these notes are identical to the minor blues scale, but the biggest difference is that the 3rd degree of the scale is major (welcome back open 2nd string!) – so the overall tonality of the scale changes.

The Mixolydian mode is a seven-note scale that contains these notes in the key of G.

G A B C D E F

As we did with the minor blues scale, let's look at this scale in open position.

 6-K - G MIXOLYDIAN MODE IN OPEN POSITION:
Track #42

This Mixolydian mode, or major-blues scale is found up at the 12th fret as well. However, you'll see that in order to play all of the scale notes, you'll actually need to venture all the way down to the 7th fret at one point. The 7th fret, 4th string could also be played as 14th fret, 5th string.

 6-L - G MIXOLYDIAN MODE AT 12TH FRET:
Track #43

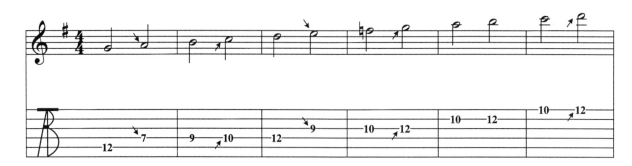

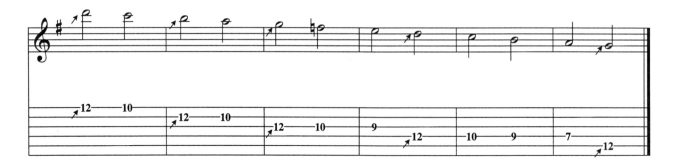

Now we'll look at the major-blues, or Mixolydian mode on each string.

6-M - G Mixolydian Mode on the 6th String:

6-N - G Mixolydian Mode on the 4th String:

6-O - G Mixolydian Mode on the 1st String:

6-P - G Mixolydian Mode on the 5th String:

45

6-Q - G MIXOLYDIAN MODE ON THE 3ʳᵈ STRING:

6-R - G MIXOLYDIAN MODE ON THE 2ⁿᵈ STRING:

Once you've got a grip on those modes/scales, you'll have a very strong idea of how the fretboard works. So how do you decide which scale to use? There is no simple answer – for some reason the minor based blues scale sounds great over 7th chords (which are major-based chords), as does the major-based Mixolydian scale. There are lots of great players who mix and match them all the time. If you can be aware of the scale you're playing and choose your time and place to jump into major or minor based playing, you'll find that both work well over most standard 7th-based blues progressions.

MIXING THE TWO SCALES

Another way to approach blues soloing is to emphasize the chord changes, by switching scales over different chords. Let's try a simple example of this.

> Play the G Mixolydian mode over the **I** chord.
>
> Play the minor blues scale over the **IV** chord.
>
> Play out of the 7th fret position for the **V** chord.

If you play this example unaccompanied, you will hear the chord changes happen within the notes you're playing. The reason that this works well is that the main change from G major to minor is changing the note B to B♭. In the I (G7) chord, there is a B and in the IV (C7) chord there is a B♭. Let's try this concept now over the blues progression.

The scales don't always have to be so perfectly divided up over the chords like that. Let's finish off this chapter with trying to play a little over a blues using bits and pieces from all the scales. See if you can hear the differences.

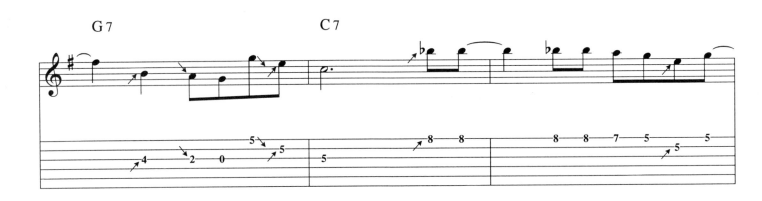

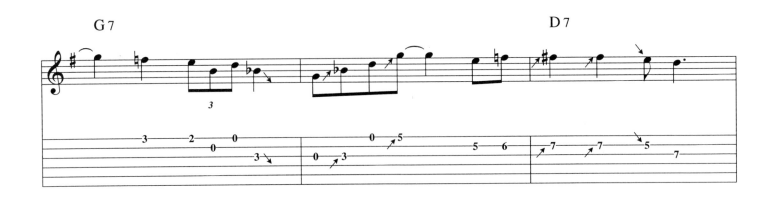

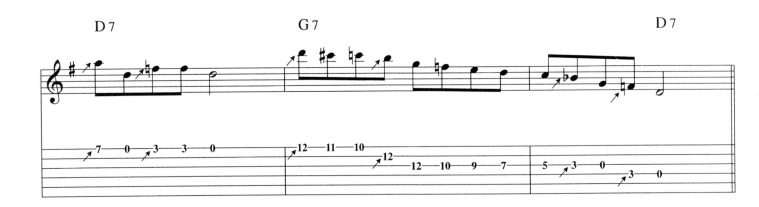

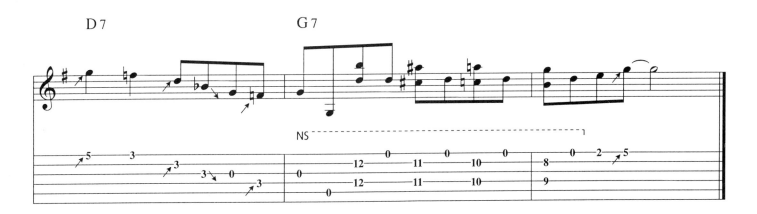

CHAPTER 7 - RHYTHMIC VARIATIONS

Part of the ability to play and improvise in any style of music is having a knowledge base of rhythmic possibilities to draw from. You can get pretty adventurous with rhythm and really add some zest to your solos by making them rhythmically exciting. In this chapter, we'll look at the basics of this and how you can incorporate it into your style.

In this chapter, I assume that you know the basics of what a bar is, that it has four beats, and have a basic understanding of quarter notes, eighth notes and their respective rests. We'll be using notes from the blues scale that you are already familiar with. Your attention should be focused on the rhythmic aspects of the exercises – the melodic content will be straight from Chapter 6. You might find a metronome useful for many of these exercises. If you're comfortable using one, set it to a slow speed to start, and then move up in speed gradually.

QUARTER AND EIGHTH NOTES

These quarter notes are all on the beat, and will be played at the same time as each click if you're using a metronome. If not, try and tap your foot in a steady rhythm to get a pulse running through your body. Remember to apply the muting techniques from Chapter 4.

7-A – QUARTER NOTES:
Track #46

Now try this one – same idea, different set of strings.

7-B – QUARTER NOTES:
Track #47

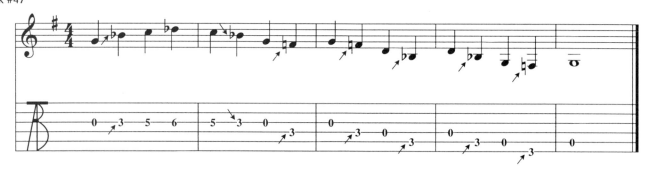

Tap your foot with the metronome so that you get your body involved – once the metronome is gone, you'll need to be your own timekeeper!

Now double the speed (of the notes you play, not the metronome!) to get 8th notes. Don't let the large clusters of notes intimidate you or trick you into playing faster than you should! The rhythm in these two examples is simple, constant, and the notes are all in order from the scales you already know.

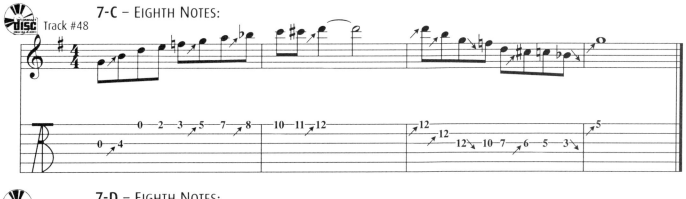

7-C – EIGHTH NOTES:
Track #48

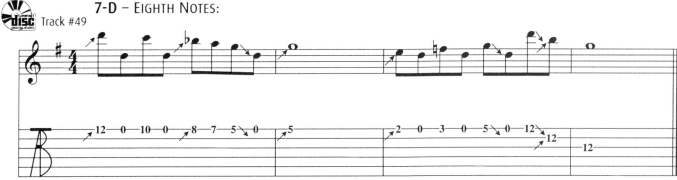

7-D – EIGHTH NOTES:
Track #49

QUARTER AND EIGHTH NOTE RESTS

Now we'll throw in some rests to spice it up a little – space is highly underrated! You can make phrases sound more exciting using syncopation (playing rhythms that are offset from the actual beat). So far, we've looked at constant streams of notes. Next, we'll yank some out. Quarter note rests would be the equivalent of one metronome click. You could work on this by playing every other note from exercises **7A** and **7B**. Eighth note rests are a little trickier...

By removing every second 8th note, we're leaving the downbeat open. These notes, except for the last one, will all fall between your foot taps (on the audio CD, I'll be emphasizing the beat with a loud foot-tap).

7-E – OFF-BEATS:
Track #50

Here's a more musical phrase using the same ideas.

7-F – OFF-BEATS
Track #51

51

And now a couple of short examples that incorporate a lot of the ideas we've been working on. Watch for all the different note values, some tied notes, quarter note rests, etc.

 7-G – EVERYTHING SO FAR:
Track #52

 7-H – MORE OF EVERYTHING SO FAR:
Track #53

Now we'll tie it all together with a blues progression, similar to what we did in Chapter 6, but spiced up with our new rhythmic concepts. Try tapping out the rests on the strings as they come along. This will keep the groove going through the spaces. The chords are written above the music for playing with accompaniment, but this will also work as a solo piece.

 7-I – 12-BAR BLUES USING RHYTHMIC VARIATIONS:
Track #54

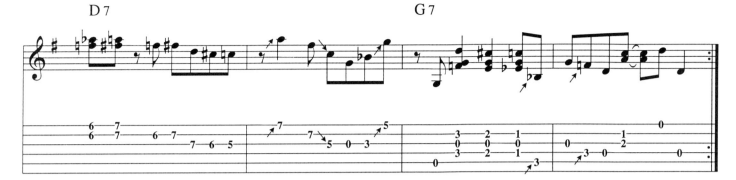

TRIPLETS

A triplet is three equal notes played in the space of two. The first kind we'll look at is quarter note triplets. In the space of two metronome clicks (or foot-taps), we'll play three equal notes.

7-J – QUARTER NOTE TRIPLETS:
Track #55

In this case, we have 8th note triplets - three equal beats in the space of two 8th notes. Try clapping the rhythm or tapping it on your leg before you try this.

7-K – EIGHTH NOTE TRIPLETS:
Track #56

Here are some more triplets, this time using pull-offs to the open strings. Use your finger instead of the slide for the very last triplet, which is a hammer-on.

7-L – TRIPLETS USING PULL-OFFS:
Track #57

And finally, this example uses notes from the blues scale but without the slide (except for the last note of bar 1 and the first note of bar 2). Try and let the fretted notes ring out along with the open strings.

7-M – TRIPLETS INCORPORATING OPEN STRINGS:
Track #58

In order to integrate triplets into your playing, you should make sure you fully understand how they work and fit into a musical phrase. Develop some exercises for yourself and practice "switching gears," or going back and forth inside of one bar between quarter notes, quarter note triplets, or 8th notes and 8th note triplets. Also, try listening for these rhythms in other people's playing – and not just guitar players! Check out some of the great trumpet, saxophone or piano players for some ideas...

Now we'll incorporate everything from this chapter, once again in the G blues progression:

7-N – BLUES PROGRESSION USING ALL RHYTHMIC VARIATIONS FROM THE CHAPTER:
Track #59

Chapter 8 – String Pairs and Melodic Options

Up to this point in the book, we've mostly looked at playing single notes. In this chapter, we'll look at the different sounds you can get by playing partial chords – mostly in the form of two notes at once, or **double stops**, as they're known in guitar-land.

Octaves

We'll start with the easiest interval to understand – the octave. Playing octaves means that you play two notes that have the same name, but one note is seven scale steps higher or lower than the other. In G tuning, there are lots of octaves to choose from. Any note you play on the 3rd string can be doubled with an octave lower by playing the same fret on the 5th string.

In this exercise, we'll play a lick on the 3rd string by itself, and then we'll play the same thing again in exercise **8-B**, but we'll add in the octave below. Use your thumb and middle finger of your right hand to play these, as in the photo.

8-A - G Lick Using Single Notes:
Track #60

56

8-B - G LICK USING OCTAVES:

Now we'll try some octaves on the D strings. We'll do these on the 1st and 4th strings, and on this set of octaves, you'll need to use the muting techniques from Chapter 4. By playing these two strings at once, you'll find that the 2nd and 3rd string will have a tendency to ring out as well. Because of this, try playing these sets of octaves with your right-hand thumb and ring finger. Mute the 3rd string with your index, and the 2nd string with your middle finger.

8-C – G LICK USING OCTAVES ON 1ST AND 4TH STRINGS:

Track #62

Now we'll move on to a tune using our stellar octave abilities...

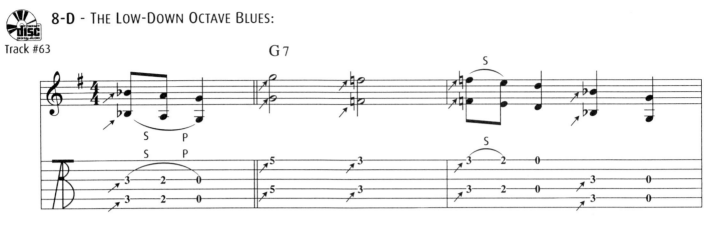

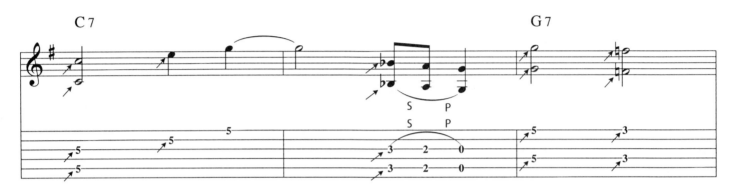

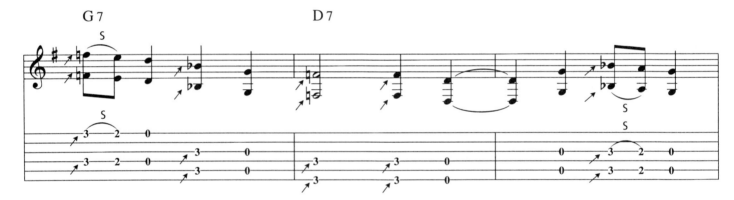

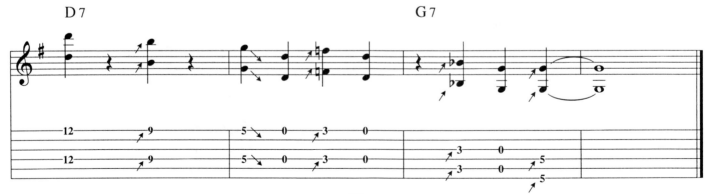

THIRDS

Thirds are a very common harmony in blues, country, Hawaiian, jazz and lots of other styles of music. There are two kinds of thirds – major and minor. From a scale point of view, you find the third by locating your first note, and then skipping a scale note (the second) and the next note of the scale is the third. On the guitar, you would locate your first note that you want to harmonize (we'll say it's the 7th fret, 3rd string) and then move up the string four frets to the 11th fret (This is equivalent to moving up two scale degrees). This note is the third. Conveniently, on the guitar, this same note is located on the 2nd string, 7th fret. So by playing the 7th fret of the 3rd and 2nd strings together, you have a major third.

8-E – MAJOR THIRD:

Because of the way this tuning works, the only pair of strings that have this type of third in the same fret is the 3rd and 2nd strings.

Thirds are a very useful sound for playing songs and soloing. To understand how they work, you should learn to harmonize the G major scale in thirds. You can do this by looking at the scale separately on the 3rd and 2nd strings.

8-F - HARMONIZING THE G SCALE ON THE 2ND AND 3RD STRINGS:

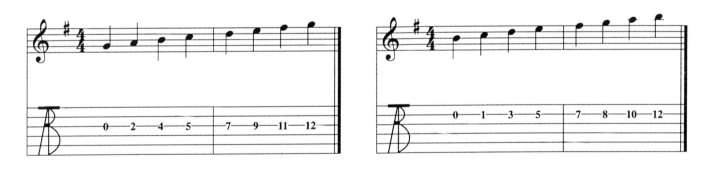

By stacking these two versions of the scale, so that the first note from bar 3 goes on top of the first note from bar 1, the second note from bar 3 goes on top of the second note from bar 1, etc. you can harmonize the entire scale. Think of this as two different fingering positions. The first is using the slide to cover the G and B strings together at the same fret. Look at 8-F to determine which double-stops would end up on the same fret – the 1st (open strings), the 4th (the 5th fret), the 5th (the 7th fret) and the 8th (the 12th fret).

For the double-stops that don't land on the same fret, you'll need to use a second fingering position. To get the second fingering position, you'll need to lower the note on the 2nd string by one fret. There is a technique to accomplish this by fretting the 2nd string behind the slide, essentially "bypassing" the slide, but that's for another book. For now, we'll just play the rest of the notes by using your 1st and 2nd left-hand fingers (no slide).

8-G - THE ENTIRE G MAJOR SCALE, HARMONIZED IN THIRDS (THE 2 VERSIONS OF THE SCALE FROM **8-F** COMBINED INTO 1):

Track #64

The other kind of thirds found in this tuning are the minor third, which falls on the 2nd and 1st strings in open-G tuning.

8-H - THE G MAJOR SCALE ON THE 1ST STRING:

Track #65

Now we'll combine these up with the notes from the 2nd string (see **8-F**). Because these thirds are minor, every time we hit a pair that isn't in the same fret, we'll have to use fingers again to move the 1st string up a fret to create a major third.

8-I - THE 1ST AND 2ND STRINGS HARMONIZED IN THIRDS IN THE KEY OF G:

Track #66

60

Now try going through these string pairs with the slide, playing one note at a time. Muting will be important here – use your right hand thumb and index finger, and be sure that as you play one string, the other is being muted (see Chapter 4).

 **8-J – PLAYING THIRDS AS INDIVIDUAL NOTES:**
Track #67

Try the same thing on the 2nd and 3rd strings.

 **8-K – THIRDS ON THE 2ND AND 3RD STRINGS:**
Track #68

Play both of these exercises ascending (up) and descending (down). Now we'll add some bluesier sounding thirds to the arsenal. These are mostly accomplished by changing certain major thirds into minor thirds.

61

8-L – ALTERING THIRDS TO GET A BLUES SOUND:
Track #69

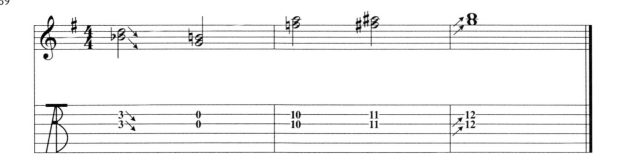

And on the 1st/2nd string pairs.

 8-M – ALTERING THIRDS ON THE 1ST AND 2ND STRINGS FOR A BLUES SOUND:
Track #70

Now let's incorporate all these types of thirds into a tune.

8-N – BLUES WITH THIRDS:
Track #71

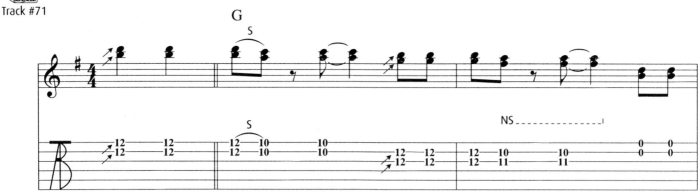

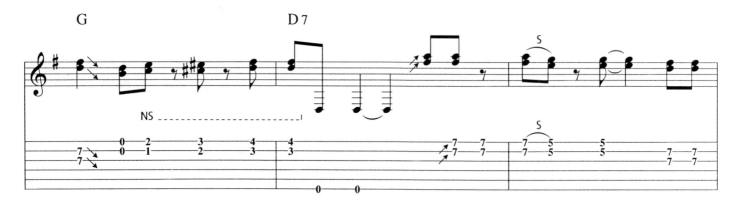

62

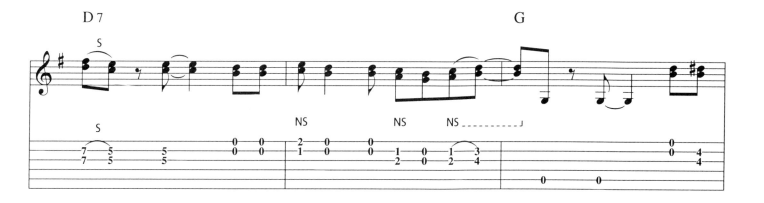

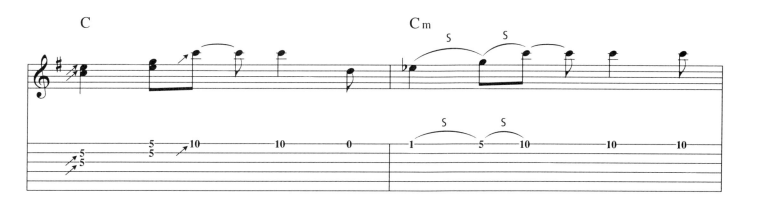

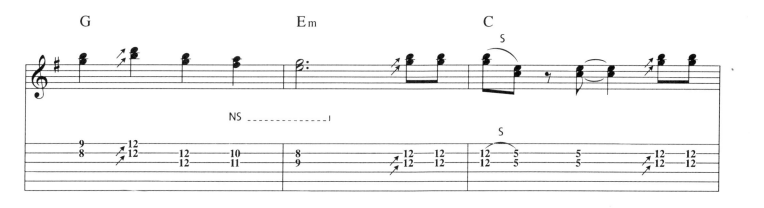

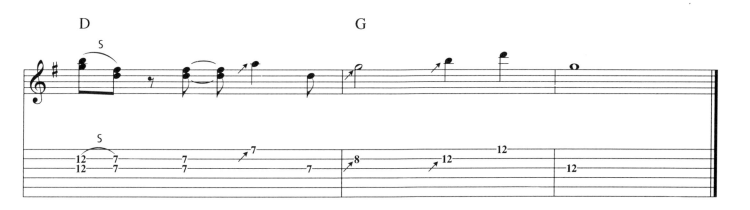

SIXTHS

Sixths are another common interval found in many different styles. Sixths played on the slide guitar will make people reach for their favorite hula outfit – they just naturally sound Hawaiian. Hawaiian and western swing guitarists developed a slide tuning that incorporated a sixth into the open chord in order to have plenty of access to them. Like thirds, there are two kinds of sixths – major and minor. To find the sixth interval on the guitar, you would locate your first note that you want to harmonize (let's say it's the 5th fret, 4th string) and then move up the string nine frets to the 14th fret to find the sixth. This note can also be found at the 5th fret, 2nd string. So once again we find ourselves with a handy interval two strings apart on the same fret.

8-O – MAJOR 6TH:

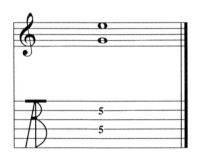

The only pair of strings that have this type of sixth in the same fret is the 4th and 2nd strings.

In keeping with the previous examples on thirds, let's take a look at the G major scale on the 4th and 2nd strings.

8-P - G MAJOR SCALE ON 4TH AND 2ND STRINGS:

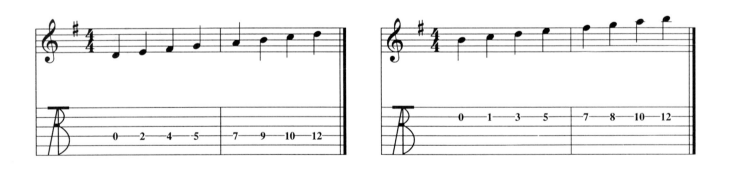

Now we'll combine them and use slide for the sixths in the same fret, and fingers for the sixths that are separated by a fret.

As with thirds, there are certain sixths that are better suited to a blues sound than the ones from the major scale. These notes are derived from a more minor sound, as well as some chromatic positions that just seem to work well. These are some examples:

 8-R
Track #73

Practice all of these sixths up and down the neck, played together and also one note at a time.

Now we'll incorporate some sixths and all of these techniques into a piece.

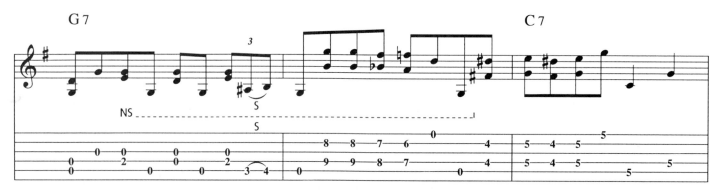

There are other intervals used in different styles of music, but to get the basics of playing blues slide, thirds, sixths and octaves are the main intervals needed.

You can take these intervals a long way – make sure to spend some time mastering the concepts and practice all of the exercises at different speeds, backwards and forwards, and as single notes and double-stops. You'll find all of these tools very useful in opening up your playing, improvising, and your musicality.

CHAPTER 9 – PLAYING SOLO

Depending on what style of music you're playing, and what performing or practicing situations you find yourself in, you might want to be able to perform as a solo slide guitarist. In this chapter, we'll look at two techniques involved in playing both a melodic and a rhythmic part together – **alternating bass**, and **deadthumbing**.

ALTERNATING BASS

One way of playing unaccompanied is with a simple alternating bass pattern. To do this, you keep your right-hand thumb playing a somewhat consistent pattern, and adding in melodic notes (played with your right-hand fingers) either at the same time as a bass note, or in between bass notes. We'll start with just a simple bass line. Your thumb will play each of these quarter notes. Try to get your foot tapping along with each of these beats.

9-A – BASIC ALTERNATING BASS PATTERN:

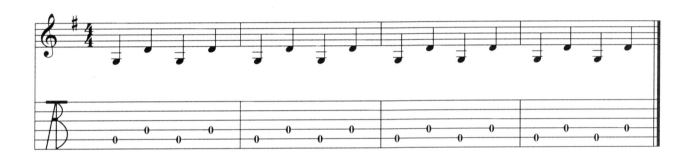

Try to **mute** the bass strings by placing your right palm on the bridge – you'll still hear the note, but the sustain will be short and punctuated. Listen for this in the audio examples.

Before moving on, make sure you can do this evenly, without speeding up, and most of all you want to be able to do this without thinking about it!

Now we'll add in some melody. On the 1st and 3rd beat of each bar, play the open 3rd string with your right-hand index finger. When you play a melody note together with a bass note, it is called **pinching**.

Track #75 **9-B** – ADDING YOUR INDEX FINGER:

Now try the opposite – play the open 3rd string on beats 2 and 4.

 9-C – ADDING YOUR INDEX FINGER ON BEATS 2 AND 4:
Track #76

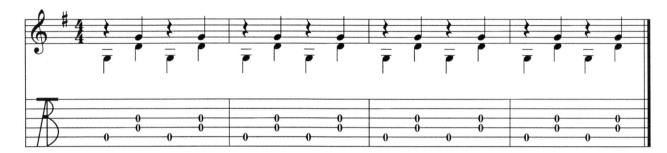

Next we'll add in some more melody. Use your right-hand index finger for the 3rd string, and your middle finger for the 2nd string. This time, each note will be pinched.

 9-D – ADDING YOUR MIDDLE FINGER:
Track #77

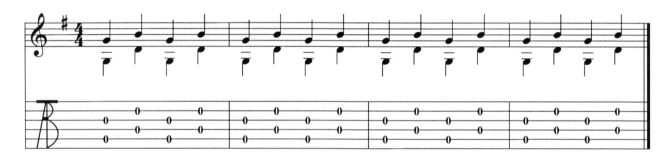

In this next exercise, we'll pinch every note again, this time adding in one more melodic note on the 1st string (use your right-hand ring finger for that one).

 9-E – ADDING YOUR RING FINGER:
Track #78

So far, all the melodic notes have been pinched on the beat, along with the thumb. Now we'll make things a bit more syncopated, and start playing melody in between the beats. This will make the music seem much faster, as there's so much more information going by, but don't get carried away and try to play this exercise too fast. The tempo and total time are the same as previous exercises, but the amount of notes in that time frame has increased.

9-F – PLAYING MELODY ON THE OFF-BEATS: Track #79

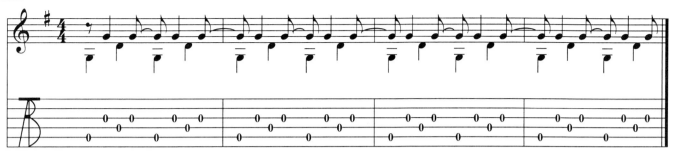

Now we'll move on in a similar fashion – adding in new melodic notes in stages.

9-G – ADDING MORE OFF-BEAT MELODY NOTES:
Track #80

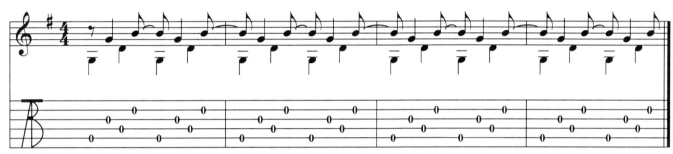

Remember to keep one right-hand finger designated to one string – index on the 3rd, middle on the 2nd, and ring on the 1st.

9-H – ALL 3 RIGHT-HAND FINGERS ON OFF-BEATS:
Track #81

Let's bring in the slide! The next two exercises are two-bar riffs that incorporate lots of the previous picking examples with slide notes. Practice these as repeating patterns.

9-I – ADDING THE SLIDE:
Track #82

In this next exercise, when you slide into the notes on the 1st string, make sure you angle the slide, so that you're still free to play the open 5th and 4th strings for the bass line. In the 2nd bar, the slide will come down on the 3rd fret, as both the bass and melody play it.

9-J – MORE WITH THE SLIDE:
Track #83

Here's a four-bar pattern that jumps from the open position to sliding at the 12th fret.

9-K – 4-BAR PATTERN WITH ALTERNATING BASS:
Track #84

Now let's apply these techniques to the other chords from the blues progression. First, the **IV** chord, using the slide at the 5th fret; Playing slide over a full five or six-string chord like this will be a good indication of how well your guitar is set up for slide. You may also have to press a little harder than normal to get these to ring out.

9-L – REPEATING PATTERN FOR THE C CHORD:
Track #85

9-M – MORE COMPLEX C CHORD PATTERN:

Here's a good transition lick, which will help you get from the **IV** chord back to the **I** chord.

9-N – TRANSITION FROM C TO G CHORDS:

Notice that while you leave the 5th fret in the 2nd half of bar 2, the picking pattern still stays the same as you venture back to the open position for the **I** chord. For the **V** chord, try exercises **9-L** and **9-M**, moved up to the 7th fret. Another way to play the **V** chord with alternating bass is to use the open 6th and 4th strings as your bass notes. Because of the way we're tuned, these notes are both D's. Since the **V** chord is a D chord, you can keep the bass pattern going on those strings and play notes on the top string with the slide angled at 45 degrees, so it doesn't interfere with your open string bass lines. Here's the minor blues scale on the 1st string, using this pattern as the bass line:

9-O – BLUES SCALE WITH ALTERNATING BASS:

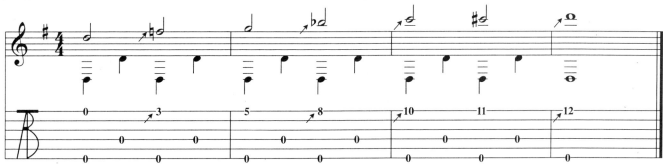

We'll now incorporate all of these concepts into a tune. You'll notice this progression is 24 bars long – it's really just a 12-bar blues again, but in order not to cram too many notes into the music, I've written it so that each bar from the 12-bar progression becomes two bars of music. Take your time with this one and try to really catch the differences between the pinched notes and the notes that fall in-between the beats.

9-P – Blues Using Alternating Bass:

G 7

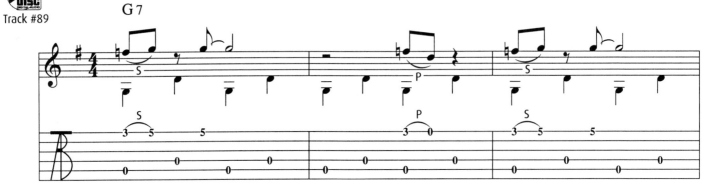

G 7

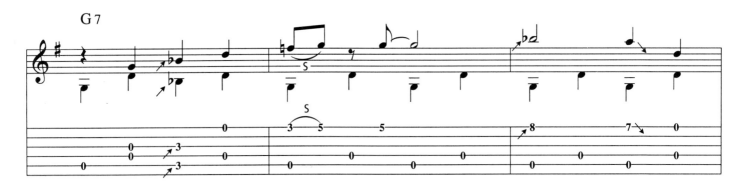

G 7   C 7

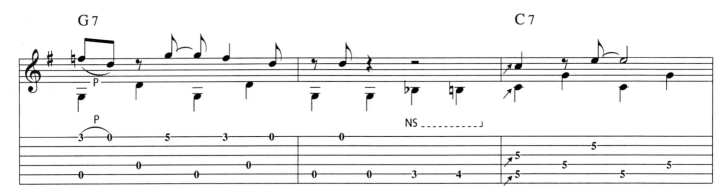

C 7

G 7

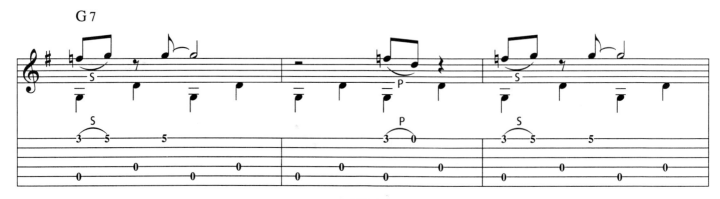

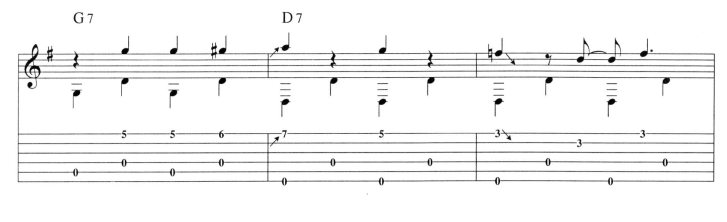

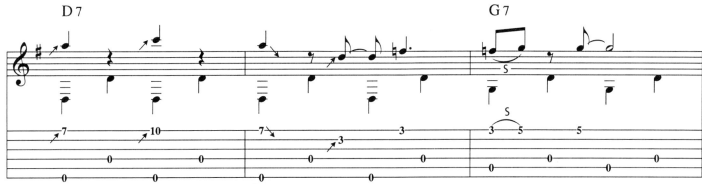

DEADTHUMBING

This technique also involves a constant bass-note pattern that keeps regular time, but instead of alternating between different notes, it generally involves staying on one note.

To get started, keep a regular bass note going on every beat with your thumb.

9-Q – BASIC DEADTHUMBING:

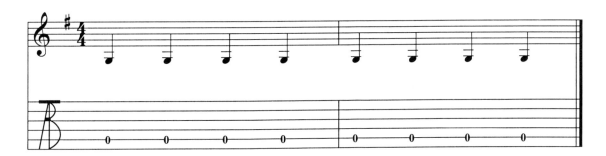

In the same way that we added to the bass with melodic notes, either pinched or in-between beats, add in some melody such as in this repeating two-bar phrase.

9-R – Deadthumbing With Simple Melody:
Track #90

These two techniques of playing a simple bass line and syncopated melody at the same time are effective means of self-accompaniment. However, these techniques can be developed to include more advanced rhythms and to involve your thumb in a more melodic fashion that to give it such a basic role as we have here. That, however, is for another book.

Deadthumbing is quite common in a lot of early country-blues and this next example is reminiscent of that style. Watch out for a few tricky rhythmic spots!

9-S – Country-Blues Style Using Deadthumb:
Track #91

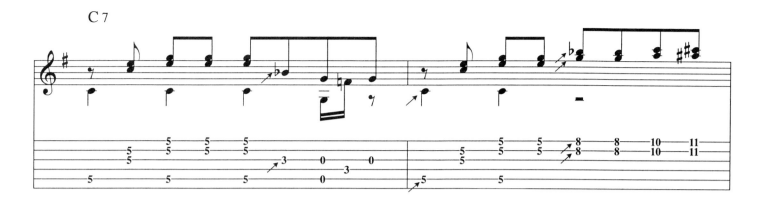

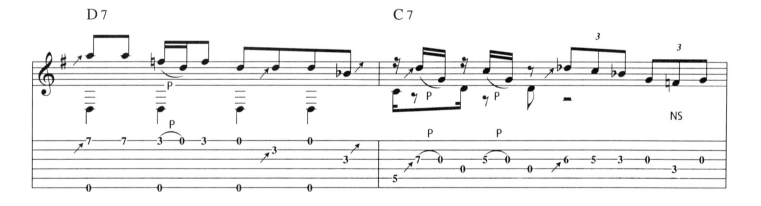

CHAPTER 10 – PLAYING IN OTHER KEYS (IN OPEN-G TUNING)

Believe it or not, there are other keys besides G, (not that you'd know it by looking through the earlier chapters!) I wanted to keep things simple in this book and not fill your head with too many scale and key variations. You are now free to take your slide prowess and explore whatever areas you choose. But first of all, let's just take a look at how you can take what you know now about playing slide and move out of the comfortable key of G.

The first thing to understand is that as soon as you leave the key of G, you are leaving some or all of the open strings behind. While this will somewhat limit you, it shouldn't scare you off from trying to play in other keys. We'll start with keys that can still use some open strings, and move on to other keys that don't.

KEY OF D

This is the second easiest key to play in when you're tuned to open G. The reasons for this are:

      1) The scales for D and G are very similar (there's really only a one-note difference in most
         of the scales)

      2) You have three open D strings on the guitar (1st, 4th and 6th)

So let's orient ourselves with the key of D. First of all let's identify and then locate the **I**, **IV**, and **V** chords.

      I chord = D (played at 7th fret)
      IV chord = G (played open or at the 12th fret)
      V chord = A (played at the 2nd fret)

Now let's take a look at the D minor blues scale and Mixolydian mode. This is the only other key that we'll go through these scales for. Because of the open strings, they're good to learn, but for any other keys, if you want to work out the scales, you should be able to figure out how to do it on your own.

D-MINOR BLUES SCALE

The D-minor blues scale, like the G version has the following notes:

      I = D
      Flat III = F
      IV = G
      Sharp IV = G♯
      V = A
      Flat VII = C

Learn it on each string – I'm not providing audio examples for these exercises, as you should be able to play these on your own.

10A – D-Minor Blues Scale on the 6th String:

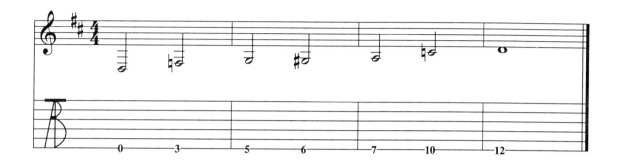

10B – D-Minor Blues Scale on the 4th String:

10C – D-Minor Blues Scale on the 1st String:

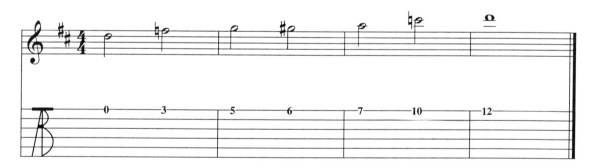

10D – D-Minor Blues Scale on the 5th String:

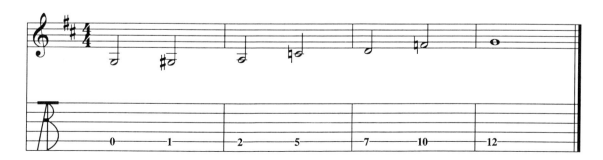

10E – D-MINOR BLUES SCALE ON THE 4TH STRING:

10F – D-MINOR BLUES SCALE ON THE 2ND STRING:

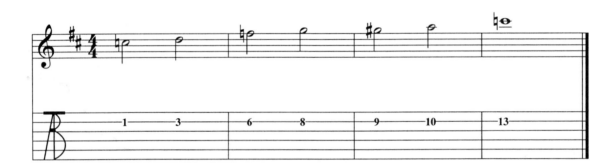

Here's an example of a melodic line using the D-minor blues scale over an eight-bar piece with no chord changes. This style of blues is typical of Blind Willie Johnson (although he would have played this in open-D tuning). The first time through (the first eight bars) will just have the melody on the 1st string – practice that section first, and then move on to the next sections, which will start hitting some of the other strings. Since this whole piece is over a D chord, you can add in some drone notes, such as the open 4th string to beef it up a little (listen for this in the audio example).

D MIXOLYDIAN MODE

The D Mixolydian mode has the following notes:

        I   = D

        II = E

        III = F♯

        IV = G

        V   = A

        VI = B

        Flat VII = C

Here's the Mixolydian mode on each string:

10-H - D MIXOLYDIAN MODE ON THE 6TH STRING:

10-I - D MIXOLYDIAN MODE ON THE 4TH STRING:

10-J - D MIXOLYDIAN MODE ON THE 1ST STRING:

10-K - D Mixolydian Mode on the 5th String:

10-L - D Mixolydian Mode on the 3rd String:

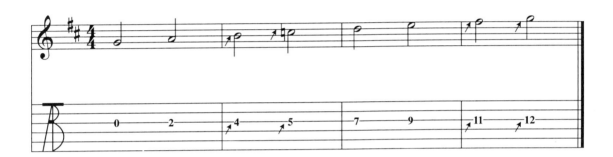

10-M -D Mixolydian Mode on the 2nd String:

Let's take a look at an example of the D Mixolydian mode in action...

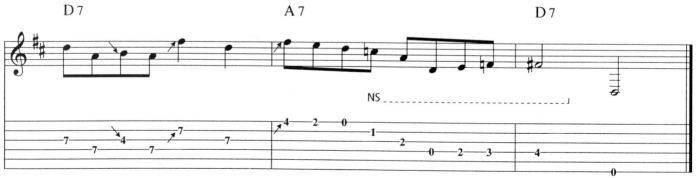

There are several variations on both the D and C tunings, as well as a number of other entirely different tunings that work well with slide. Use these exercises and examples as a starting point to explore the tunings and start experimenting with which ones feel and sound the best to you.

Here are a few variations to try out:

Open-D Family (tunings that are based on open-D)

D Minor = **D A D F A D**

D sus 2 = **D A D E A D**

D sus 4 = **D A D G A D**

Open-C Family

C sus 2 = **C G C G C D**

C sus 4 = **C G C G C F**

C Minor = **C G C G C E♭**

CD CONTENTS

Each track on the audio CD is a recording of the exercises from the chapters. Each exercise that is a full piece of music will have two versions - a slow one of just solo guitar, and then an up-tempo version with the band. Elliot Polsky plays all the drums and Andrew Downing plays the double bass.

1) Tuning Notes
2) 2-C
3) 2-E
4) 2-G
5) 3-A2 with band
6) 3-B
7) 3-C
8) 3-D
9) 3-E
10) 3-F
11) 3-G slow and with band
12) 3-H
13) 3-I
14) 3-J
15) 3-K with improvising
16) 3-L with improvising
17) 4-A
18) 4-B
19) 4-C
20) 4-D
21) 4-E
22) 4-F
23) 4-G
24) 4-H
25) 4-I
26) 4-J slow and with band
27) 4-K slow and with band
28) 5-A
29) 5-B
30) 5-C
31) 5-D
32) 5-E
33) 5-L slow and with band

34) 5-M slow and with band
35) 5-O
36) 5-P
37) 5-Q
38) 5-R slow and with band
39) 6-B
40) 6-C
41) 6-J slow and with band
42) 6-K
43) 6-L
44) 6-S slow and with band
45) 6-T slow and with band
46) 7-A
47) 7-B
48) 7-C
49) 7-D
50) 7-E
51) 7-F
52) 7-G
53) 7-H
54) 7-I slow and with band
55) 7-J
56) 7-K
57) 7-L
58) 7-M
59) 7-N slow and with band
60) 8-A
61) 8-B
62) 8-C
63) 8-D slow and with band
64) 8-G
65) 8-H
66) 8-I

67) 8-J
68) 8-K
69) 8-L
70) 8-M
71) 8-N slow and with band
72) 8-Q
73) 8-R
74) 8-S slow and with band
75) 9-B
76) 9-C
77) 9-D
78) 9-E
79) 9-F
80) 9-G
81) 9-H
82) 9-I
83) 9-J
84) 9-K
85) 9-L
86) 9-M
87) 9-N
88) 9-O
89) 9-P slow and fast
90) 9-R
91) 9-S slow and fast
92) 10-G slow and with band
93) 10-N slow and with band
94) 10-O slow and with band
95) 10-P slow and with band
96) 10-Q slow and with band
97) 11-E slow and with band
98) 11-H slow and with band